P9-BYU-014

By Joan Walsh Anglund

A FRIEND IS SOMEONE WHO LIKES YOU
THE BRAVE COWBOY
LOOK OUT THE WINDOW
LOVE IS A SPECIAL WAY OF FEELING
IN A PUMPKIN SHELL
COWBOY AND HIS FRIEND
CHRISTMAS IS A TIME OF GIVING
NIBBLE NIBBLE MOUSEKIN
SPRING IS A NEW BEGINNING
COWBOY'S SECRET LIFE
A POCKETFUL OF PROVERBS
CHILDHOOD IS A TIME OF INNOCENCE
A BOOK OF GOOD TIDINGS
WHAT COLOR IS LOVE?
A YEAR IS ROUND
A IS FOR ALWAYS
MORNING IS A LITTLE CHILD
DO YOU LOVE SOMEONE?
THE COWBOY'S CHRISTMAS
A CHILD'S BOOK OF OLD NURSERY RHYMES
A BIRTHDAY BOOK
THE CHRISTMAS COOKIE BOOK
THE JOAN WALSH ANGLUND STORYBOOK
EMILY AND ADAM
A CHRISTMAS BOOK
TEDDY BEAR TALES

For Adults
A CUP OF SUN
A SLICE OF SNOW
GOODBYE, YESTERDAY
THE CIRCLE OF THE SPIRIT

A BOOK OF POETRY

joan walsh anglund

RANDOM HOUSE NEW YORK

For Margaret K. McElderry,
my dear friend and first editor,
with love and gratitude for
all our years together

Copyright © 1987 by Joan Walsh Anglund. All rights reserved under International and
Pan-American Copyright Conventions. Published in the United States by Random House, Inc.,
New York, and simultaneously in Canada by Random House of Canada Limited, Toronto.

Library of Congress Cataloging-in-Publication Data:
Anglund, Joan Walsh. The Joan Walsh Anglund book of poetry. SUMMARY: A collection
of poems on a variety of topics including shoes, blueberries, nature, and seasons.
1. Children's poetry, American. [1. American poetry] I. Title. II. Title: Book of poems.
PS3551.N47A6   1987   811'.54   87-4429   ISBN: 0-394-88465-5 (trade);
0-394-98465-X (lib. bdg.)

Manufactured in the United States of America   1 2 3 4 5 6 7 8 9 0

A TABLE OF CONTENTS

BLUEBERRIES

Blueberries in the morning,
Blueberries at night,
Blueberries in the afternoon,
any time is right!

We picked blueberries over the hill,
picking and eating till we had our fill,
then over the hill and down the road,
and into the beach house,
with our blueberry load.

Blueberry tarts and blueberry pie,
Blueberries with cream
    and sugar piled high,
Blueberries sweet in a bowl or a jar...
    but blueberry muffins
        are BEST by far!

A little lady, all in gray,
        hurried through my house today.
She paused a while
        to eat a crumb;
She squeaked a bit,
        she scurried some,
And then as quickly
        as she came
She disappeared! . . . But just the same,
I'm awfully glad she didn't stay . . .
        that little lady . . . all in gray.

How quickly
        grows our Baby
Soon he is *so* tall!
But though I feed my Dolly
        she doesn't grow at all!

Something's happened!
    It happened to *me*!
Yesterday,
    I was only three.
But when today
    came through the door,
Suddenly,
    I turned to FOUR!

The birds are singing
          in the trees;
On every breeze,
          their sweet notes glisten;
The birds,
          they do not sing to *me,*
They sing to life!
          But I may *listen*!

Oh, it's out to visit the pony!

And it's out to see the cow!

And it's out to pet the rabbit
and her new little bunnies now.

And I'll stop to see the lambkins
that are frolicking in the sun . . .

Oh! it's out to visit *anyone* . . .
when there's housework to be done!

If I were a train
        I would travel along
With a chug-chug cough
        and a clickety song.

If I were a choo-choo
        upon a track
I'd hurry to places
        and then hurry back.

And all of the while
        I'd huff and I'd puff
Till maybe by dusk
        when I'd had quite enough,

Then into the roundhouse
        I'd go for a snooze.
If *I* were a train
        that's what I'd choose!

Gentle Sister, Little Brother,
     do not quarrel
         . . . for time is brief.

Surely all this silly squabbling
     can only lead
         to tears and grief.

You've been given
     one another
         to help you through
         the days you live.

So put your arms
     around each other
         . . . join hands, and hearts,
     and then
         Forgive!

Naughty Puppy!
　　Now *sit* there!

Don't climb up
　　upon this chair.

Please don't chew
　　my nice new shoe.

It's not the proper
　　thing to do!

Leave that dinner plate
　　alone!
Here's a Special Doggie-Bone.

Catch the stick!
　　Now bring it back.

Oh! You've left
        a spilled-milk track . . .
All across the kitchen floor.

Puppy! Don't
        run out that door!

Now, just look!
        . . . Those dirty paws,
caked with mud
        and bits of straw.

Naughty Puppy!
        You can't be . . .
Up here in bed
        with Bear and Me.

Puppy! Puppy!
        What to do?
You're oh-so-sweet,
        but you're NAUGHTY,
        too!

If *I* were a Queen
   and *you* were a King,
     wouldn't that be
       a lovely thing?

Or
should we be Friends,
    always side by side;
Which way is best?
     . . . I just can't decide!

No Friend
    more faithful
       than a Book!

Spring
    is only
       a Robin
   away!

Each seed is a Beginning
of some later blossom, fair,
But I wonder as we tuck them
in the cozy darkness there,
Do they whisper, in their mud-beds,
of the flowers they shall be?
"She, a Larkspur!
You, a Daisy!

But a Sunflower
is what *I'll* be!"

How nice that toes
      are always there,
Whether in socks
      or whether quite bare.
Tied up in boots
      or sandals or shoes,
Toes always go with me
      wherever I choose!
It's pleasant for them
      to wiggle about
In all sorts of places,
      and when I go out . . .
To splash in the puddle
      or dance in the rain,
My toes seem to like it . . .
      they never complain.
Or when like a rose,
      I stand in the mud
And squish it so gently
      . . . like a cow with her cud.
My toes are delighted,
      they're comfy and cool;
They do quite prefer it
      to walking to school!
Like ten good children
      in neat little rows
My toes are quite happy
      . . . as one might suppose.

There is a Little Place I Know
        that no one seems to find
Where I can do just as I please
        . . . and never have to mind
And never have to listen
        and do the things they say
So in that Little Place I Know
        is where I like to stay!

When you're in a forest
        or when you're at the zoo,
It is not wise to hug a bear,
        it's not the thing to do.

But when you're in the nursery
    and it's time
    to dim the light,
Oh! *then*
        to hug a TEDDY BEAR
        really seems
        quite right!

No Buttercup
        too small
    to hold
            its share
            of Sunlight.

So many creatures,
　　　　　all so small,
live in our garden,
　　　　　climb the wall,
nest 'neath the roses,
　　　　　hide 'midst the buds,
creep through the grasses,
　　　　　burrow through mud;
So many creatures
　　　　　we seldom meet
. . . a World, unnoticed,
　　　　　lies just at our feet!

We went to Emily's beach today;
    we walked among the dunes.
We filled our pails with sea shells
    that held such happy tunes.
We watched seagulls and cooled our toes
    in frothy waves of blue,
We went to Emily's beach today...
    what a pleasant thing to do!

With every wave
the Sea continues
a long green story
that never ends.

Kitty, Kitty
        . . . coat of silk,
lazily lapping
        creamy milk.

Kitty, Kitty
        . . . luncheon done,
curls to nap
        in the noonday sun.

Autumn is an Apple
hanging way up high

Winter is a Snowflake
quickly blowing by

Springtime is a Crocus
awakening in the Sun

but
Summer is Vacation!

Oh, Summertime
is
Fun!

A gardener must be prepared
to work,

and water, and weed,
and never shirk

from tasks like hoeing
. . . till the job is complete.

And then, Lucky Gardener
. . . be prepared

to *eat!*

We packed away my things today,
     the things with which I used to play.
The little dolls, the house, and all . . .
     the tiny pictures on the wall.
The little lamp with paper shade,
     the furniture that Daddy made.
The curtains Mother sewed one day;
     each tiny thing is packed away.
In tissue, wrapped, within a box,
     up in the attic, carefully locked.
Until the day another child,
     by curiosity beguiled,
Shall, eager-hearted, climb that stair
     to lift the lid and find them there.

The night is dark
    and the goblins are out,
and witches and black cats
    are prowling about.

And costumed creatures,
    the strangest I've seen,
are knocking on doors
    'cause tonight's *Halloween!*

If I were a pumpkin
    I'd not be a pie,
    but a Jack-o'-lantern
    on a post, up high.

I'd not stay a "nobody"
    at home on the vine,
    but put on a wide grin,
    and oh! how I'd *shine*!

See my new shoes!
      so bright and so black;

A ribbon in front,
      a tap at the back.

They're only for parties . . .
      Mother tucks them away.

But sometimes I find them!
      Then I dance and I play!

I click and I clatter
      all down the hall;

Oh *I* love my new shoes!
      but *Dad* doesn't at *all*!

Why must Timothy
     constantly mutter
about messy things
     like peanut butter?

Why must he long
     for jams and jellies
. . . chocolate candies
     with caramel bellies?

Oh, *why* does he pine
     for the stickiest goo
. . . great pots of honey
     dripping like glue?

Doesn't he quite realize
     that proper children's
     ways are wise?

Their clothes are neat,
     their hands are clean,
     with not a speck
     of sweets between
Their little fingers?
     Not a bit!
Cleanliness?
     He's not heard of it!

But oh, how pleasant
     life *could* be
    for Mommy dear, *if* Timothy
could mend his ways
     and appetite,
shun all sweets,
     and do things right.

Then, happy their home
     and their family,
and thinner by far
     dear Timothy!

A THANKSGIVING THOUGHT

It's time for the turkey,
     It's time for the pies,
It's time for the glow
        in each child's eyes.

It's time for our prayer
     of Thanksgiving
          to start;
It's time for Love
     to abide in our hearts!

There is a church
    we live beside
It has a stillness
    all inside
Till Sunday morning
    bright and clear,
  it speaks
    with bells
      . . . for *all* to hear!

There's a whirlwind
with tousled hair.

It swirls around our house and stair.

It leaves a trail wherever it goes

of broken toys and dirty clothes.

Nothing it touches is quite the same

. . . can you guess
the whirlwind's name?

To Bed, to Bed!
      It's off to Bed.
What? . . . you'd like
      some milk, instead?
Oh, you'd like
      a cookie, too.
And one for Bear,
      that makes two.
Brush your teeth?
      . . . of course, you're right.
Plump the pillow,
      leave on the light.
Tuck in the blankets
      . . . now they're straight,
One more kiss
      . . . it's getting late.
A lullaby?
      I'll stroke your brow.
A little dream
      is coming now.
Look how softly
      dreams can creep,
See, my angel
      . . . you're sound asleep!

What says it's time for Christmas?
      Is it the merry bells?
Or is it when the kitchen
      is sweet with spicy smells?

Or do we know when packages
      are hiding in the hall?
Or when the tree, all tinseled,
      stands rainbow-bright and tall?

Is it caroling . . . or candy canes,
      or teddy bears, or drums . . .

Is it dolls, or toys, or puddings,
      that tell when Christmas comes?

What says *best* "It's Christmas!"
      Is it all these things?
Or is it when we feel the Love
      that Christmas always brings?

I have a Friend
in red and white
who sometimes comes to call.

He visits on a Wintery Night
when softest snowflakes fall.

He does not knock
nor make a noise,

But, oh! He leaves such lovely toys,
I know he loves us *all*!

Oh, Friendly Moon
    that has watched me all my life

Oh, Gentle Moon
    that knew me when I first began

Oh, Yellow Moon
    that sees me now
        . . . shine brightly upon me.

Oh, Moon
    who watches *all* things

    . . . who visits with the stars
        and the planets
        and the universe

. . . who intimately knows the owl
        and skittery bat

. . . who nightly sees
    raccoon
        and mouse
           and cat,

    Moon, who is Friend
        with the Darkness,
        kind Prince of all the Night,

Oh, Moon . . . Look down now
   and wash the hills with silver,
   smile the lake awake,
   dance along the treetops
      when *I* run.

Gather stars up
   in your silver arms
   and spill them down
      to me.

Moon! Guard the Night
   and never sleep!

   And while *we* dream,
      oh, Moon!

   Watch over *us,*
      the little ones!

I have a little furry friend
Who waits upon my bed.
All through the afternoon
    not a Teddy-word is said.
All through the evening story
    so solemn and so still,
He guards the patchwork valley,
    he keeps the pillow hill.
But then, when all the lights are out
    and Mother goes away,
He tells the best of Dreamy-tales
    . . . and suddenly,
it's DAY!